EJ Schmid, Eleonore.

Hare's Christmas gift.

14 DAY BOOK

FOR NORMA ELISA
Understanding follows amazement.

Copyright © 2000 by Nord-Süd Verlag AG, Gossau Zürich, Switzerland
First published in Switzerland under the title *Der Weihnachtshase*
English translation copyright © 2000 by North-South Books Inc.
All rights reserved. No part of this book may be reproduced or utilized in any
form or by any means, electronic or mechanical, including photocopying,
recording, or any information storage and retrieval system,
without permission in writing from the publisher.
First published in the United States, Great Britain, Canada,
Australia, and New Zealand in 2000 by North-South Books,
an imprint of Nord-Süd Verlag AG, Gossau Zürich, Switzerland.
Distributed in the United States by North-South Books Inc., New York.
Library of Congress Cataloging-in-Publication Data is available.
A CIP catalogue record for this book is available from The British Library.
ISBN 0-7358-1376-0 (TRADE BINDING) 10 9 8 7 6 5 4 3 2 1
ISBN 0-7358-1377-9 (LIBRARY BINDING) 10 9 8 7 6 5 4 3 2 1
For more information about our books, and the authors and artists
who create them, visit our web site: www.northsouth.com
Printed in Belgium

HARE'S CHRISTMAS GIFT

BY ELEONORE SCHMID

TRANSLATED BY ROSEMARY LANNING

NORTH-SOUTH BOOKS · NEW YORK · LONDON

It was almost sunset. Shadows lengthened and a cool breeze rustled the dry grass. Soon the first stars would appear.

A timid young hare woke from his rest and sniffed the cool evening air. All should be quiet now. It would be safe to leave his hiding place and search for sweet herbs to eat.

He stopped suddenly and listened. Tonight something was different.
The birds had not flown home to roost. The air was still full of their song.

Butterflies were on the wing, and small animals chattered excitedly.
What could be happening?

Animals large and small hurried toward the little hare.

He leapt out of their way, but the animals passed by without a glance at him.

Then the hare saw a man and a woman heading toward the stable.
They looked very tired.

But why were they going to the stable? The hare had never seen people
there at night. And why were the animals following them?

The hare hopped a little closer. Light streamed from the stable door, and the man came out to draw water from the well.

He spoke quietly to the animals. They did not shy away, but listened attentively. Had they no fear of the stranger?

The animals hurried away to collect branches, roots, and twigs.
The birds helped too, and the mice gathered bunches of dry grass.

Was the man going to build a nest? wondered the hare.
He would have liked to go and see, but he did not dare.

At last curiosity overcame the little hare. He crept closer.
The man had built a fire.

Butterflies danced in the flickering firelight. Doves cooed, bats swooped low, and birds carried downy feathers into the stable.

High above glittered a star, brighter than any the hare had ever seen.
Now silence and peace settled over the countryside.

The light in the stable shone brighter still. The animals gathered at the door, patiently waiting their turn to look inside.

As they turned away, their eyes shone. For a moment they stood still, as if in a dream. Then they walked slowly back into the night.

What had they seen? The hare hopped from side to side, uncertainly.
Should he have gone with them?

How he wished he had! Then he heard a rustle.
A mouse came pattering past.

"What did you see in the stable?" the hare asked shyly.
The mouse spoke of a newborn child, a child so special that she could
not describe him. The hare must go and see for himself, she said.

So the timid hare gathered all his courage and ran to the stable.

Outside, he stopped and listened. All was quiet.
The hare hopped into the stable and looked around him.

There, on a bed of dry grass and feathers, lay a newborn child. The hare gazed at him. How cold the baby must be, with no fur to keep him warm. The hare crept into the manger and snuggled close to the child.

Feeling the soft fur under his hand, the child smiled in his sleep. The hare felt no fear now, only joy and contentment, knowing that he too had given a gift—the gift of his warmth—to this special child.